Twelve Days of Fruitcake

written by

Nancy Hill

November 2012
10 9 8 7 6 5 4 3 2 1

This book is fiction. Any resemblance to living people or dolls is purely coincidental.

Send permission requests to:
Irish Eyes Productions
5735 SW Brugger
Portland, OR 97219

To Cody and Dusty, naturally

Days of Christmas

Day One 7

Day Two 12

Day Three 18

Day Four 23

Day Five 34

Day Six 44

Day Seven 49

Day Eight 54

Day Nine 57

Day Ten 61

Day Eleven 66

Day Twelve 69

Day One

Arella Hazelton holds her freshly baked fruitcake, plump and the perfect shade of deep, rich brown, to the window to let the candied fruit sparkle in the afternoon sun. Frost has already formed on the thin windowpanes of her crowded kitchen, lightening her mood. She loves the lacy patterns frost creates, and cold doesn't much bother her.

The sun bounces off the fruitcake, magnifying the number of sweet cherries and pineapples she mixed into the sticky, dark dough the day before. She is never stingy with the fruit—that's where fruitcakes go wrong. The more surprising flavors that burst through the dense cake, the better the revelations. Most people don't understand that fruitcakes are mysterious, full of secrets and unspoken possibilities. There can never be enough of such things.

Arella spent so much of her food budget on the ingredients for her cake that she will live on scrambled eggs and a big pot of bean soup for the rest of the month. She doesn't mind. This is the only gift

she has to give and she's made it spectacular. She even splurged on brandy, an ingredient she believes makes or breaks a fruitcake.

She places her fruitcake inside a tin she has saved to bear her gift. The container is quite old. Once golden with a ring of pears and holly surrounding a picture of a wintry scene too faded to decipher anymore—although a deer can clearly be seen in just the right light—the tin has lost its glory. But Arella believes age adds character, and she is certain the random chips and scratches on the lid only make the slightly dented container more memorable.

Jokes about fruitcakes don't trouble Arella. She's even secretly pleased that many people are afraid to try something as quirky as fruitcake, with every bite a surprise. As a child that had meant she had the whole fruitcake her grandmother made her family all to herself. Not that she'd ever eaten it all at once. That is another good thing about fruitcakes. They last. They don't harden or crumble or, worse, grow moldy. They are meant to be savored, slim piece by slim piece.

The only person Arella knows who loves fruitcake as much as she does is Bea, her neighbor. Arella draws her eyebrows together as she puts on a navy blue wool cardigan and picks up the tin to deliver to Bea. In the time it takes her to walk to her door, Arella recalls her first meeting with her neighbor.

Two years ago it was. Arella hadn't a friend in the world. She'd been placed into this tiny apartment—senior housing—by a social

worker after a developer had bought the apartment building Arella had called home for thirty years. It took the developer less than four months to tear down her building and construct co-ops where her home had once stood. The tenants had been disbursed throughout the city. They may not have been great pals, but they were neighbors, and there had been a rhythm to their community. They knew each other's comings and goings, could hear their states of health through the thin walls, knew their heartaches and joys by unintentionally overheard laughter and sobs. And while few of them knew specific details of each other's lives and kept to themselves, they shared an unspoken agreement that they would help each other if the need arose. When they ran into each other in the stairwells or long halls, they smiled on good days and at least managed to nod when times were rough. If there were disagreements, they simply ignored each other.

The first evening Arella had been brought to this old folks' apartment building, Bea had shown up at her door before Linda Dell could give her a complete tour of her new apartment. According to the glossy business card Linda had handed her, Linda was a settlement agent. Arella had tried to persuade the social worker she didn't need to be escorted to her new place by this—or any other—settlement agent, but it seemed she no longer had any say about what went on in her life. The Senior Services Department had even moved all Arella's furniture in and unpacked everything before she

had a chance to decide where things should go. The apartment she herself would occupy had been under renovation the day she had been allowed to preview her new home, so the manager had shown her an empty apartment that was a mirror-image of where she would live. Once in her actual space, everything seemed backward, adding to her unease.

As Arella had stood with Linda and tried to grasp the new arrangement of doors and windows, short hallways and small rooms, a woman she'd never seen before marched into the cramped living room, stepped between Arella and Linda, and with hands on her hips informed Arella, "I've made a big casserole and expect you to help me eat it."

While Arella mulled this over, Bea continued, "And I've got two cold beers chilling in the icebox. If we're going to hear each other's bathroom sounds, we may as well get acquainted."

Bea had taken Arella's arm as if they'd been friends since grade school. "I'm Bea, by the way," she'd said as she tugged Arella toward the door. Arella turned to Linda long enough to catch her expression, the settlement agent's too-wide mouth gaping open like a fish. Arella hadn't seen Linda again.

Arella's thoughts return to the present as she steps into the hallway and locks the apartment door. Bea has been sick for the past few months. The doctors are still running tests; every result ruling out

something they can cure. Bea's future is bleak. Several doctors have told her that frankly, the time has come for her to put her affairs in order. But Bea hasn't enough strength to do much more than make coffee and sit in an overstuffed chair by the window watching stray dogs chase feral cats.

Arella refuses to let the tears stinging her eyes slip down her cheeks. It will not do to let Bea see her cry.

She crosses the corridor and sings *Deck the Halls* in her still-sweet voice until Bea answers her knock. She doesn't let her voice falter, even though her friend is already little more than a ghost.

Day Two

Bea hasn't told Cindy, her daughter-in-law, about her health problems. What would be the point? For the past twenty-two years, Cindy has only seen Bea once a year for an early Christmas dinner. They always meet at a fancy restaurant of Cindy's choice. Bea understands that they don't meet more often. Cindy is a very busy women. At first it was hard for Bea to see Cindy at all, each visit opening up a wound too deep to heal. But over the years, Bea has come to look forward to this dinner. Now, rather than being devastated by the reminder of her loss, she feels Cindy is her only connection with the best part of her life.

Bea long ago let go of the fact that if it weren't for Cindy, Jim and the boys would have been in a safe car. Instead, Cindy had asked Jim if he could take the kids on ahead without her. "I'd love just twenty minutes to myself to take a bath. Your mother will understand."

Jim had taken Cindy's mini-van, leaving his Honda for Cindy to drive. His car had snow tires; Cindy hadn't had time to take her

vehicle in to have the tires changed. Jim had promised he'd take it to the garage for her that weekend. But the snow hadn't waited. It had been coming down on and off all day, making the roads slippery in unexpected places.

Just a few blocks from Bea's house Jim had swerved to miss a dog. The car skidded into oncoming traffic across lightly packed snow. Both Jim and the two little boys—three-year-old identical twins—had been killed on contact.

Nothing was ever the same for Bea, but it was Cindy who had changed the most. She never allowed herself a minute's rest, as if taking even a second for herself would cause a catastrophe. She filled every moment with activity, never taking time to enjoy the fruits of her labor before diving into another project. Another cause.

Bea had clapped her hands in relief three years after the accident when Cindy phoned to tell her she was engaged. Cindy was young. She needed to heal. Perhaps when she had children again, she'd remember to slow down and enjoy life now and then.

Instead, Cindy had doubled her efforts to take on more than anyone could reasonably handle and, worse yet, she believed everything had to be perfect. Each year she found new projects to take on, more people to help, more things to plant in her garden. Not even the demands of a husband and child, a stressful career, or volunteer work could cure her of her compulsion to get everything

right. And as her daughter grew older, Cindy involved herself in her daughter's school, the PTA, and served as the team mother for almost every team her daughter played on.

This need seems to sizzle her nerve endings, driving her to do more, more, more. All of it without a misstep. Without error.

As Bea steps into the cab Cindy thoughtfully called to take her to their Christmas dinner, she loses her grip on the fruitcake. She catches it just before it tumbles to the curb.

Bea has been too sick to go out shopping and has worried about not having a gift for Cindy. Even though Cindy has everything she could possibly need, Cindy might read something unintended into a change in their tradition of exchanging gifts. But now, thanks to her thoughtful neighbor, she has something to give Cindy after all. Arella will never know she's passed the fruitcake on to someone else. And even if she were to find out, she would understand.

Cindy is seated when Bea arrives at the restaurant. Its magazine-perfect holiday ambiance takes away Bea's small bit of ambivalence. She watches Cindy rise as she follows the hostess to the table. Cindy's fair hair is shorter than usual and she wears a sprig of white holly over her left ear. As the light streams through the window, Bea catches her breath. In her wintry white dress, Cindy looks like a young bride again.

"You simply never age," Cindy compliments Bea when the two women are comfortably seated. "How do you do it?"

"Liver pills," Bea teases, grateful that Cindy has chosen to ignore the weight loss, the dark circles under her eyes. "Lots and lots of them. You can't imagine."

They order and as they meander through their meal, they chat about things neither of them care much about—the weather, the cost of postage, an episode on a long-running TV show they both enjoy. Bea names several books she's read lately, asking Cindy if she's happened to read any of them. Cindy majored in literature. Bea recalls how Jim loved to tease them about the hours they spent discussing characters in books as if they knew them personally.

Cindy shakes her head. "I can't remember the last time I had a chance to open a book."

Bea sees stress lines in Cindy's face, the weariness in her eyes. She wants to ask what's wrong, but just as Cindy has tactfully not commented on Bea's appearance, she does not remark on these signs that Cindy is under too much pressure.

Do these Christmas dinners add more stress? Bea wonders. It is the busiest time of the year, and perhaps the memories these annual dinners bring back are still difficult to manage.

Almost exactly an hour later, Cindy puts her debit card on the silver tray the waiter discreetly slides onto the table and hands Bea a gift beautifully wrapped in gold foil. Burgundy velvet ribbons cascade off to one side.

Bea, in turn, hands Cindy the fruitcake.

Cindy's eyes smile for the first time since Bea sat down across from her. "Fruitcake!" she cries. She eases the lid off the tin and inhales.

"This is the same one you always made for Jim, isn't it?" Cindy continues. "Our first Christmas together—we had just started dating—Jim insisted I try some. I told him I didn't care for fruitcake at all, but he promised yours would be different."

Again, Cindy inhales the sweetness. "I can't thank you enough," she tells Bea. "It's like having him with us still." She pauses. "Do you think it's wrong that I still miss him?"

Bea reaches across the table and takes Cindy's hand. "It's good to harken back to the things that were important to us," Bea replies, her face softening into a smile. "Sometimes the pressures of the moment make us forget to slow down and remember the pleasures of the past." She doesn't even consider admitting she has not made the fruitcake. Nor does she remind Cindy that Cindy never cared for her fruitcake until she'd had an unexpected craving for it when she was pregnant.

They hug at the door. Bea is fairly certain her ill health means they will not meet again. There are so many things she would like to say, but does not want to intrude. "I couldn't have asked for a better daughter-in-law," she whispers, holding Cindy close for longer than she ever has before.

And she means it. Long ago Jim confessed he had almost decided to stop dating Cindy when she hadn't liked Bea's fruitcake. Bea had laughed and told her son he'd never find anyone to marry if that was his test. "It's enough that she even tried a piece, you knucklehead," she'd said.

Now it's enough to know Cindy still remembers the significance of the fruitcake, even if the story has changed with time. What hadn't? What wouldn't?

When Cindy helps Bea into the cab, their eyes meet and hold until the cab driver impatiently asks for the second time where Bea's headed. For the briefest of moments, Bea and Cindy are together as they were thirty years ago, both expecting wonderful things to come.

And as the cab pulls away from the curb, Bea is stunned to find herself thinking, believing even, that wonderful things could still be up ahead.

Day Three

Cindy always has too much to do, too many people who need her help. What would it be like to sit and enjoy a good book? She once loved to read, but now she has to be content with the thrill she gets from buying books from the Internet, savoring plans to actually read them "this time." But between her family, her job, and volunteering with three different organizations, "this time" remains elusive.

She calls her daughter on her cell phone to see what last minute details she might need help with before the high school Christmas pageant. Even though her daughter is almost seventeen, she still relies on Cindy to take care of the tedious details of her life. Like father, like daughter.

Cindy slams the brakes to avoid a car that stops unexpectedly in front of her. Great, another delay. She's already running late. All the top management will be at the office Christmas party, and there's no room for error. Every year Cindy volunteers to organize the

party; every year she swears it will be the last time she takes on the responsibility. Not only are the party preparations taxing, but the board members, particularly Jeannette Bamford, tend to be highly demanding, as if the party is for them alone.

Cindy pulls her dark green hybrid car into the private parking spot she earned two years ago by being the employee of the month for six consecutive months. She's proud of this spot. It's the only recognition she's received for her tireless efforts. She has never been promoted, although her job duties increase every year. She has trained many people hired into better paying positions than hers and watched younger women rise in the company because they possess self-promotion skills Cindy lacks. She organizes fund raisers for non-profits whenever one of the board members passes the responsibility on to her, knowing full well the board member will be the one to receive the accolades. She doesn't mind. The non-profits all have worthy missions. She graciously accepts the nickname Old Faithful, even though she inwardly cringes whenever she hears it.

Turning off her car, she reaches for her purse and the present for the gift exchange. Her face falls. She's forgotten the present. She sees it clearly in her head, lying right there where she left it on the buffet by the front door. How could she have been so absentminded? She checks her watch and lets out a small cry. There isn't time to get back to the house and still put the finishing touches on the boardroom.

She swivels around to face the back seat, foolishly hoping she absentmindedly put the gift there instead of on the passenger seat beside her where she generally places things she's taking to the office.

But no. Nothing.

Maybe it fell off and slid under the seat? She leans forward and reaches under it. "Ah-ha! Got you!" she cries as her hand connects with a solid object. She strains to retrieve it, but when she see it, her heart sinks.

The fruitcake. She'd forgotten to bring it into the house after her dinner with Bea the previous evening.

She rests her head against the steering wheel to consider her options. It comes to her then. How obvious! She'll bring the fruitcake to the gift exchange. Nothing wrong with that. Bea's fruitcakes have won prizes. They're delicious. Fresh. Moist. Fragrant. It will more than suffice.

Her anxiety eases when the party gets underway. Her efforts have not been in vain. From the decorations to the buffet, the entertainment to the gift table, she has set the stage magnificently. When Vern Jackson, the CEO, gives his speech, his list of thank-yous goes on for a good five minutes. Her name does not come up. Later he'll pull her aside and tell her it goes without saying that they couldn't do without her. "That list is so long already," he'll say. He does this every year.

When the applause dies down, Vern directs everyone's attention to the gift exchange. "Cindy? Where are you? You're up!" he says into

the microphone, putting his hand over his eyes as if he has to search for her.

He spots her standing by the gift exchange table, exactly where he expects her to be, and adds, "Oh, there you are. I was wondering where you'd run off to again."

This brings the predictable laugh. Jeannette Bamford places herself next to Cindy to help hand out gifts.

Thomas Hugh, a fairly young man recently assigned several highly visible ad campaigns, ends up with the fruitcake. He pats his stomach. "Just what I need, a few more pounds," he jokes.

"Whoever brought that?" Jeannette Bamford asks so only Cindy can hear. "I'd expect our staff to have a little more culture than to bring such a tacky gift."

Cindy's first reaction is shame. She should have gone back home for the gift she'd intended to bring. How could she have brought such an inappropriate gift? But then, unexpectedly, her mortification turns to anger. Tacky gift? Jeannette has no idea the value of that fruitcake.

Observing Cindy's distress, Jeannette gives a hollow laugh and says, "Oh dear, it wasn't you, was it? Of course it was. Anyway, so sorry. I'm sure it's delicious. At least I would hope so."

When Cindy's shock renders her speechless, Jeannette adds, "Not to be rude, but there are still gifts to pass out. It's time to move on."

The words resonate deeply inside Cindy, and with clarity she has not felt in years, she hands the microphone to Jeannette, "Yes. It is indeed time to move on. I resign," she says, her voice strong and certain. The mic picks up her every word.

Conversation comes to a halt. Cindy feels all eyes on her as she glides across the floor with her head held high and exits the boardroom like a queen. She stops in her office for her coat and glances briefly at the familiar items in the small room. Is there something she should bring home? But no, of course not. Her office has always been perfectly professional. Items from home do not belong in the workplace.

As she crosses the parking lot, she reaches inside her purse for her keys. Out of habit, she checks her cell phone for messages. Three. No doubt people wanting her help.

She turns off her phone. Whatever it is can wait. Or the callers can figure out solutions for themselves. Tonight, she's going home and cuddling up with a good book. And when she finishes it, she's going to call Bea and ask her if she'd like to start a book club with her. A book club of two sounds just about the perfect number.

Day Four

4:45 p.m.

Thomas checks his watch. Good. Still plenty of time. It won't do to be late this evening. Not after last night. And certainly not on the evening he makes his annual pronouncement of love for his wife. What will he compare Alice to tonight? It'd better be good. Very good.

He'd expected his promotion to double his workload. He's one of the youngest copywriters in the agency's history to advance so far so fast. If he wants to continue to rise, he has to prove he'll give his all. But these sixty hour weeks are wearing on him. And Alice. He cringes at the thought of the previous evening.

He checks the calendar on his computer, browses the task list. Not too bad. If he hurries, he can cut the list in half before 5:30 and still have plenty of time to stop off for just the right wine. He shrugs off the guilty feeling that comparing his love for Alice to wine isn't

exactly original. He'll find a label with art that will inspire something unexpected and it'll be perfect. He sure wouldn't be handling two premiere accounts if his copy writing skills weren't among the best in the business. He knows how to make words sing. And Alice deserves an entire aria. Where would he be—who would he be—without her?

5:30 p.m.

Thomas puts a check mark by another item on his task list. Darn. Only three items completed. He has five more to go if he wants to get to the half-way point before he calls it a day. Sure, there's nothing that can't wait until morning, but he likes to start the day with fewer than ten items on his list.

His eyes trail to Alice's photograph. Stunning. Gorgeous. A real knock out from all angles. But thinking of her in terms of her physical appearance doesn't begin to capture the essence of her, for beyond the most incredible body and beautiful face he has ever seen, is a spirit so joyful that in her presence, anything and everything is possible. Her imagination is beyond compare, and considering he works in a creative field, he has met more than his share of people whose thoughts know no limits. Her grasp of intellectual matters is likewise amazing, her compassion for others brings tears to his eyes, and her cooking—well, that alone could steal a man's heart. But it is her infectious laughter he most loves. Although now he can barely remember the sound of it.

He scowls. Is he responsible for muting it?

They'd waited until he'd settled into his career to get married. Alice hadn't minded. In fact, she wasn't a big fan of marriage. Her own parents had been miserable with each other, and as a child she had vowed she would never be like them. Thomas and Alice had had a good laugh over that. Of course they would know nothing but happiness together. Their love could survive anything.

But even Thomas has to admit that things are slipping. Not his love for Alice, of course, but the time they spend together seems full of chores instead of exploration. Their conversations have become an exchange of information about who will be where, when, instead of a sharing about what goes on in their hearts and souls.

Alice had brought things to a head the night before when he'd forgotten all about their dinner plans. Alice's best friend, Virginia, and her new husband, Todd, had been in town for a brief visit. The newlyweds had made time for dinner with Alice and Thomas, but the plans had slipped his mind. Virginia and Todd were at the airport to catch their flight by the time Thomas had come home. Alice had turned her head to the side when he'd tried to kiss her.

"Our lives have become a what-might-have-been movie," she'd said, no traces of laughter in her tone. "We're about to hit the third act where everything falls apart."

He'd pretended to take her remark lightly. "What are you talking

about, honey? Everything's going our way. Your freelance work is rolling in. I'm well on my way up to getting my name etched on the agency's door. We have our home. We've got that trip to Hawaii coming up in three months. Not a penny of it on a charge card, I might add. Nothing's falling apart here. I'm sorry I spaced out dinner. You could have called and reminded me."

She hadn't dignified his efforts to turn the tables by responding. She'd told him when they first met that they wouldn't be each other's keepers, and never once had she broken that rule.

"If you don't want to be together any more, just say so," she'd said as they settled into bed. She pulled the blankets high under her chin. "Things change. Life changes. We all change. I understand that. What I don't understand is pretending things are fine when they're not."

They hadn't said much more after that, but Thomas had stayed awake most of the night wondering what he could do to prove to her that she was every bit as important to him as she'd always been. For now, though, he had to balance their marriage with other things that were important to him. Like his career.

He'd gotten up early and made breakfast. Scrambled eggs on toast, her favorite. Over coffee, he made a point of asking her what the day held.

"Mine?" she'd asked.

"Ours," he'd replied, reaching across the table and running his finger lightly down her wrist. "I'm going to do my best to leave the office no later than six. How about if we go to dinner? Someplace full of holiday cheer."

"Like to your parents' for their annual family feast, you mean?"

"Exactly," he said, grinning. "What time are we supposed to be there?"

They both knew his parents' feast had totally slipped his mind, but his response was so quick and such an obvious cover up that Alice couldn't help but laugh. Oh, what a wonderful sound.

"Seven."

"Sharp," he promised. He squeezed her hand. No words passed between them, but in that touch, they both knew he was promising he would continue the ritual of doing what he called "spilling his guts" to his whole family about his love for her.

Softening, she'd said, "How about if you just meet me at your parents' house? I'll go over early and help get things ready."

He was lucky Alice got along so well with his parents. Not everybody did. Including his own sister. What was her problem, anyway? But he didn't have time to think about that.

He stops reflecting on his precarious situation and scans the task list for a couple of quick things he can do. He finds two that require no more than a brief email. There are three that won't take much

longer than a few minutes each. He glances at the time at the edge of his computer screen. He can get all five tasks done by six o'clock for sure. There will still be time to find that perfect label on that perfect bottle of wine.

6 p.m.

Determined not to let her unhappiness ruin her in-laws' dinner—or feast, as her mother-in-law insists on calling it—Alice tries to shut out her thoughts as she squeezes the lemon for the Caesar salad dressing. But that doesn't still her racing heart. She's made up her mind. She'd meant it when she'd said all those years ago that she would never stay in a marriage like her parents had endured. She and Thomas aren't there yet, but their marriage is clearly headed in that direction. She can't remember the last time the only thing that mattered was the two of them.

Just like her father, Thomas is seldom home anymore. Worse, he's late. Always, always late. A sure sign of indifference. Leaving Thomas will break her heart, but so will watching their marriage become nothing more than a tedious habit.

Their brief exchange at breakfast has given her a little hope. But words are easy—especially for Thomas. If he is late again tonight, if this dinner with his family isn't important enough for him to arrive on time, then she will know their time together has run its course.

It was during this family feast eight years ago that Thomas has stood up, tapped his fork on his wine glass, and announced he had found his soulmate.

"I have an announcement to make. I have finally met someone who is too incredible for metaphor. In fact, she will become the metaphor for all that is beautiful and wonderful. I love her more than Romeo loved Juliet, more than Lancelot loved Guinevere, more than Antony loved Cleopatra, and more than Rhett loved Scarlett. There's more, but I want to save some metaphors for the future because I plan to spend the rest of my life raving about my love for Alice," he'd gushed. Even his father's eyes had teared up.

Since then, Thomas has created metaphors for his love for Alice at every family feast. And so if he is not on time for the occasion of his annual pronouncement of love, she will know his heart is no longer hers.

6:10 p.m.

Thomas turns his computer screen off and pushes away from his desk. Still time to spare, to find that very perfect wine label that will make his metaphor sparkle. Hmmm....perhaps he should select a good bottle of champagne.

The phone rings. He waits for caller ID to come up before he decides whether or not to answer. Office hours ended over an hour

ago, so it's doubtful it's a client. Maybe his mother needs him to stop and pick something up. He groans when he sees who it is. He hooks his foot around his desk chair and pulls it back out.

"Matthew Moreland," he says into the phone. "You caught me headed out the door. But hey, I've always got time for you."

He doesn't, of course. But Matthew is a huge client, and they're in the middle of a killer deal. He'll take Matthew's calls morning, noon, or night. His future could depend on it.

6:25 p.m.

Will Matthew ever end this conversation? Thomas wonders.

He checks his watch again and groans. He has exactly thirty-five minutes to make it to his parents' house. Knowing it might be a career limiting move (a CLM as it is known in his agency), he cuts Matthew off.

"I'm sorry to do this, Matthew, but I'm running behind schedule. I'll give you a call first thing tomorrow morning. I'll set up an early breakfast meeting." He names Matthew's favorite restaurant, but Matthew is not so easily put off.

"Hold your horses there, son. There's still a couple more things I want to talk about now."

"Seriously, Matthew, I hate to do this, but I absolutely have to sign off. I can't give you another minute just now."

"Hot date?" Matthew's voice is terse.

"Exactly," he says. "With the most wonderful woman in the world. See you at eight tomorrow? I'll call and make reservations."

He doesn't wait for a reply. Without even stopping to put on his coat, he runs out of his office and down the hall. He chooses the stairs instead of the elevator, knowing it could take a full two minutes for the elevator to reach his floor. He sprints across the parking lot, hits the button on his key ring to unlock the car door, jumps inside, and speeds off.

Luck is on his side. The traffic has thinned out to practically nothing. He checks his watch. Twenty minutes to seven. As long as traffic holds and he continues to hit most of the lights green, he might even make it with a couple of minutes to spare.

6:52 p.m.

Alice watches the minutes tick away. Eight minutes before seven. She shakes her head. Her marriage is doomed. She slips into a chair and buries her head in her hands. She'll never get through this night without tears. But she has to. Somehow, she promises herself, she will find the strength.

6:56 p.m.

"Yahoo!" Thomas yells, slowing for his final turn. "I'll make it!"

But then it hits him. The wine! He forgot all about it. He can't show up without the perfect bottle of wine with the perfect label to

use for this year's metaphor. Why did he wait for the last minute for something so important? In previous years, he'd planned exactly what to say weeks in advance.

How could he do this to Alice?

He can't. It will only take a few minutes to grab a bottle of wine. There's a store just a few blocks away. Surely she won't hold it against him if he's a few minutes late. Five, ten, at the most. He can find the perfect label in that time. Something romantic and mysterious. Something that illustrates promise while also showing endurance. Something time cannot change. But will that be enough to make up for once again being late?

With a quick look in the rearview mirror and in both directions, he swings his car around, moving so fast that everything on the passenger seat flies off onto the floor. Something hits him hard in the knee and rolls beneath his foot, jamming against the accelerator.

He pulls over to the curb and reaches down for it.

His distress turns to delight as he pulls the object off the floor. "Yahoo!" he shouts again, kissing the fruitcake tin. "You're it, baby. You saved my life, you sweet thing!"

6:59 p.m.

Alice stares at the kitchen clock, willing time to freeze. One minute left. The moment has arrived. She will honor her promise to herself.

Her mother-in-law breezes through the door. "Don't tell me we're going have to start dinner without that son of mine," she says. "Well, come join the rest of us. No sense in letting the food get cold."

As Alice turns toward the dining room, light fills the kitchen. Headlights!

A glance at the clock shows ten seconds to spare!

Brushing back tears of relief, Alice watches Thomas throw open the car door. He kicks it closed and sprints up the sidewalk, something round tucked under his arm.

She opens the door and steps out to meet him. He hears her laughter before he sees her.

"You made it," she cries.

"Bearing a fruitcake of great joy," he replies, sweeping her into his arms. Who cares if the mashed potatoes get a little cold and his mother gets a little irritated? It's Alice, after all, who matters.

His love for her is like a fruitcake. It never gets stale, never loses its flavor, is full of unexpected pleasures, and has survived all the tests of time. A little corny. But true.

Which is all that matters.

Day Five

Sondra yanks her comforter back and practically throws herself into bed. She can't believe it. But what did she expect? Her mother just couldn't help herself. Meddle, meddle, meddle. She can't bear the fact that Sondra isn't married. Isn't giving her grandchildren. Oh, her poor mother just feels so left out when her friends pull up darling pictures of their darling children on their darling cell phones and she doesn't have any darling grandchildren to show in return. Well, let her pressure Thomas about that one. He's been married what—seven years now —and still no babies? You'd think with his perfect marriage, he and Alice would have half a dozen kids by now. Just thinking of how Thomas and his gorgeous wife couldn't keep their hands off each other all evening makes her stomach tighten into crooked rows of disorderly knots. What a couple of show offs. And of course when her mother brought up the inevitable baby question, Thomas had hinted that they might just need to set another place at the table next year. "No promises," he'd said. "But it could happen."

The evening had shown possibilities when her father had come home with an unexpected guest. Someone from work. Alex Franklin. Her mother had appeared less than pleased. Surprises unsettled her, but she had accepted the new addition to their family gathering gracefully when Sondra's father had explained the circumstances.

"He was all set to go home to visit his parents for the holidays, but they both came down with some rare respiratory illness. They're in the hospital in isolation. They can't have any visitors because their resistance to other illnesses is so low. It's not fatal, so he's handling it well. He was headed out to the airport when he got the call. He looked so forlorn, I thought he might appreciate a distraction."

Her mother had quietly set an extra place opposite Sondra, and Sondra found her eyes often straying across the table to Alex during dinner. He had a remarkable ability to keep his worries about his parents to himself. His eyes twinkled when he laughed, and he appeared genuinely interested in Sondra's work as a research scientist. Most men found her career choice off-putting.

After dinner, he'd asked her if she wanted to step outside to have a look at the stars. Talk about a corny line. But effective. Very effective.

They'd taken their drinks to the terrace. "Your father has been telling me about you since he first walked into my firm and we shook hands," Alex had said. "It's hard to get him to focus on business for two seconds. Not that I mind, of course."

Sondra had been momentarily thrown off. "Your firm?" she had asked, confused. "I thought you two worked together."

He'd laughed. "Not exactly. We work in an office in the same building, but I'm in stocks. Carter, Robbins, and Franklin."

"Are you the Franklin?"

"That would be my father. Me, I'm the son who took the path of least resistance and followed my dad's orders to major in economics and join his firm. But I'm finding it's not really for me."

Still trying to make sense of her father's actual connection with Alex now that she knew they didn't work together, Sondra had asked, "My father is investing in stocks?" Her father had always thought stocks far too risky. This didn't make sense.

"Actually, to quote him, he's making an investment in his daughter's future," Alex replied.

Sondra felt the veins in her temple fill with blood. "Tell me," she asked, "do the doctors think your parents will be out of the hospital by New Year's?"

His perplexed expression gave her the answer.

"They've done it again!" she said, tightening her hold on her drink so fiercely she wouldn't have been surprised if she broke the glass. "They just can't stop meddling in my life."

As if on cue, her mother stepped onto the porch carrying a bottle of brandy in one hand and that silly fruitcake Thomas had brought

in the other. Her mother, of course, had been immensely charmed with that goofy metaphor about fruitcake and love.

"It's awfully cold out here," her mother had said cheerfully. "How about a little brandy to warm you up? Here, Sondra, hold this fruitcake for me before I drop it. I thought a slice might go well with brandy."

Sondra had nearly snatched the tin out of her mother's hand. "Oh, Mom, give it a rest, will you? I don't have time for this. Now if you'll excuse me, I have some reports to write."

She hadn't bothered to tell anyone goodbye. She'd stormed off to her car and tossed the fruitcake on the passenger seat, cringing when her tires squealed as she turned out of the driveway.

Now Sondra tosses and turns with such frustration that her comforter ends up hopelessly tangled. Her efforts to straighten it out only makes it worse. Finally, she jumps out of bed, grabs her pillow and comforter and stomps into the living room.

She searches for a late night TV show that will lull her to sleep. Or at least, she hopes, will make images of Alex stop dancing in her head.

Morning

Sondra pulls out of her driveway before the sun rises. She's always one of the first to arrive at the research lab. And the last to leave. Her mother's voice comes through so clearly she might as well be in the

car with her. "You need a real life, Sondra. All work and no play will mean a lonely old age."

Lonely old age? How about a lonely young age? But what's the alternative? Dating has provided her with more misery than company. And besides, even if she could convince herself that not everybody was like Barry, who had been married; or Greg, who had turned out to be on parole for assaulting his former girlfriend; or Mark, the reporter who had dated her thinking he could sweet talk confidential research results out of her, where would she even meet someone?

In a bar? Hook up with some loser boozer? Now there's a good start.

Online? No, thank you. Trusting that someone is telling the truth on some dating site is like believing in Santa Claus.

She nearly runs a red light and then sails right through a stop sign at an intersections she's been through hundreds of time. What is happening to her?

Over tired? Sure. That must be it. And then there are unanswered questions from the previous night, and questions eat away at any scientist. For instance, when exactly would her parents have told her the truth? There was no doubt they were in on it together. What had they told Alex about her? They'd probably tricked him as well. Did they really think he'd be interested in dating the daughter of a pair of liars?

As if all these thoughts aren't enough to make her fume, there's also an annoying smidgen of regret that she'd stormed out before she gave Alex a chance. Well, she could forget about him now. She'd clearly blown it, she reminds herself for the hundredth time as she pulls into the parking lot.

Shaking her head as if to clear it of thought, she reaches for her door handle with her left hand and flings her other hand out toward the passenger seat for her purse.

"Ouch!" she shouts as her index finger connects with something hard. Good thing long nails are impossible in her line of work or she would have broken it clear down to the cuticle.

Turning to see what dared get in her way on this bad mood of a morning, her eyes land on the fruitcake tin.

What had made her take it with her last night, anyway? She could add that to the list of dumb things she'd done.

She grabs it up along with her purse and heads into her office. She'll put the fruitcake out at lunch for her coworkers. She does *not* need a reminder of her misbehavior.

By mid-morning, Sondra's eyes seem to be able to focus on nothing but the fruitcake. She'd set it on her windowsill, the only clear spot in the lab. Maybe she should move it. She has a habit of

looking out the window whenever she needs to think. But her tasks this morning aren't complicated, so why does she keep looking toward the window? It must be the tin. The faded colors give it a bit of glamour. By some kind of magic, its age seems to make it vibrate with charm. So fine. She'll keep the tin and put the fruitcake out for her coworkers.

An hour later, Sondra looks up from her report as the sound of laughter and chatter take over the hallway. The lunch exodus has begun.

Just a few more minutes and she'll make her way to the company cafeteria, too. Her stomach is growling and nothing interesting is happening under the microscope. She scans the list of samples left for her to examine. Good grief! She isn't even half-way through it yet. Her concentration, usually impenetrable, is certainly failing her today. Every little thing distracts her.

Like that ridiculous tin. She could swear it twinkles at her.

Like Alex's eyes the night before.

Darn it. Why had she been such an idiot? Who knows, it might have been something good. Maybe he would have been the prince after her army of hopping frogs.

Now she'll never know.

But wait! She knows where he works. She can call and apologize.

No. That could be awkward for both of them.

Okay, then, she'll send him a note.

But what will she say?

Again, the tin catches her eye.

That's it!

She crosses the floor to her desk, opens the top drawer, and takes out a piece of her personal note paper. "Accept this as an apology for my bad behavior last night. How inconsiderate of me to have taken the fruitcake before you had a piece." She signs with a flourish, picks up her phone, and dials the courier's number.

Quitting time

On the way out of the office, Alex stops at the reception desk to pick up his packages. At this time of year, he, like everyone in the firm, is flooded with token gifts for services rendered. As in making the gift givers lots of money, he thinks ruefully. Why did everything have to be about money? How nice it would be if someone cared about something besides wealth.

He usually asks the receptionist to pass his gifts on to someone she knows or to keep them for herself. The last thing he needs is another pen set, a mug stuffed with exotic coffee beans, a box of expensive chocolates, or, heaven forbid, another fruitcake.

And wouldn't you know it? There it is. A fruitcake.

But not just any fruitcake. This appears to be very same one that Mr. Hugh's daughter had stomped off with the night before. Boy, what a relief to see what an ill-tempered woman she was before he'd actually asked for her phone number. He'd been right on the verge of making yet another mistake in the romance department.

Then again, maybe it's only the tin that looks familiar. Fruitcakes often come in tins. It could be from any number of people.

Curious, he reaches for it and opens the card taped to the lid.

Well, what do you know? At least Sondra Hugh had the good manners to apologize. He tells himself that he, in turn, needs to have the good manners to thank her.

Without stopping to consider who might be listening—gossip is a hot commodity in this firm—he calls Mr. Hugh and asks if he happens to have his daughter's number handy. Mr. Hugh is only too happy to oblige.

Final minutes in the lab

Sondra scowls as her cell phone vibrates across her desk. Ten more minutes, and she'll be done. She's tempted to ignore the call, but it could be her boss.

She picks up the phone and glances at the number. Good. She doesn't recognize it. No need to respond.

Moments later, her phone buzzes again. A text message this time.

Now what? She has to finish her report. She needs to go home. She wants to regroup. To sleep. She's been a mess all afternoon, wondering what Alex will think about that fruitcake. Maybe she shouldn't have sent it at all.

Too late now. With a sigh, she picks up the phone to check the text message. A slow grin crosses her face as she reads, "Thanks for the fruitcake, but it's too early for dessert. Want to grab some dinner with me first? We can swap stories about interfering parents."

All traces of irritation flee as Sondra's phone rings yet again and she sees the unfamiliar number reappear. She has a feeling this number will become very dear to her.

With a smile, she puts the phone to her ear. Already Alex's hello sounds as familiar to her as her cat's meow.

Day Six

Gus is filthy. Climbing under a house to fix pipes does that. But he doesn't mind. In fact, he sees the mud as a sign that his life has taken a turn for the better. It means he's working, earning money. Not a lot, but he isn't about to complain. Bless Father Beckingworth.

Last year at this time Gus was on drugs. Bad ones. Not that any are good, maybe, but these were the worst of the worst. Not just dangerous, but the quality was bad, too, which meant he never had his fill of them. So he found things to steal. Bless Father Beckingworth.

A church always has things around, and Father Beckingworth believes that if anybody needs to steal from a church, they must really need the money, so he never presses charges or calls the police when there is a theft. He keeps the really holy things locked up. Bless Father Beckingworth.

Not much longer than a year ago, Gus had a pretty steady small income from the candle boxes. You could count on women—especially the old ones—to always have someone to light a candle

for. It was such a woman thing to do, always thinking of others. So why not take their candle money? Wouldn't they want to help him? Besides, they were probably just lighting candles for some husband they'd hounded to an early grave anyway. Why did men bother to get married? So he helped himself regularly to the candle money. At least it paid for a fifth of whiskey. Or a few joints. Depending on his mood. But then one dismal, rainy Saturday Father Beckingworth walked in on him with his hand in the candle box. The priest hadn't been mad. "Let's talk," Father Beckingworth had said. And that had been the beginning of Gus mending his ways. Bless Father Beckingworth.

Gus has been clean and sober for coming up to thirteen months now. His life has changed. He is dating, even. A very lovely lady, a widow, whose husband was killed committing a robbery. She sure seems to be one of the good women Father Beckingworth tells him is out there. She wants a good man this time, and he is there to be that man. It's been hard getting a job, and the one he's found barely pays the bills, but Father Beckingworth sends extra handyman jobs his way whenever he can. Like this plumbing job. Right before Christmas the money is going to come in very handy. He'll be able to get his lady's gift out of layaway. Bless Father Beckingworth.

He wishes he could buy Father Beckingworth something to show his appreciation. But even if he had any extra money, what could he buy a priest? A coffee mug with a picture of an angel? Maybe he

can afford one of those. But that's a pretty cheap present for a man like Father Beckingworth. A nice wallet would be better. Even priests need one. As he washes his hands after fixing the pipe, he wonders if the man who lives in this house might have an extra wallet made of real leather laying around someplace. Probably one that's never been used. It's a nice house. Real nice. Everything about it says this guy has money. He surely has a wallet he never uses any more. Heck, maybe he even left some money in it and forgot about it. If Gus happened to find it, he'd be able to do something with the forgotten money sitting in the wallet not doing anybody one lick of good. He'd be able to show Father Beckingworth his gratitude and could even buy his lady an even nicer present than the necklace he's been paying off on layaway—like a pair of earrings to go with it.

Half way up the steps to the bedroom, Gus pauses. Father Beckingworth wouldn't like him stealing. Even if it is for a good cause. So Father Beckingworth will have to go without a present.

Especially because just as he goes back down the steps, the back door opens and in comes the owner of the house. A young guy all spiffed up after a day at the office, not a drop of sweat in sight. Gus bets he has several extra wallets around.

The man holds out his hand. "I'm Alex Franklin," he says. "I sure appreciate you coming over here on such short notice. I'm the least handy guy in the world. I hate to admit it, but I can't even find a stud

when I want to hang a picture. Sure glad Father Beckingworth knew about you. He's a great guy, isn't he? I've known him since I was an altar boy."

"Bless Father Beckingworth," Gus replies. "Well, the job's done and everything's in good order."

"What do I owe you?"

Gus thinks about jacking up his price, but this guy Alex is a decent sort. He doesn't insist on checking things out himself or asking a bunch of questions to try to show he could have done the job better himself.

"Sixty dollars will do it," Gus says, padding the bill just a tiny bit.

Alex hands him two fifties. "Keep the change," he says. "Merry Christmas."

Gus smiles, shakes Alex's hand warmly. "Hey, thanks, man."

Alex is touched by this gratitude. It'd be awkward to give him more money. His eye falls on the fruitcake tin. He picks it up.

"Merry Christmas," he repeats and hands Gus the fruitcake for emphasis.

Gus is thrilled. Not only will he have enough to buy earrings to set off the necklace for his new lady friend, he now also has something to give Father Beckingworth. A fruitcake. Instead of being in jail for stealing this guy's wallet, losing his lady, disappointing Father Beckingworth, and being so bummed he goes back to bad drugs and cheap booze, he'll be able to give Father Beckingworth a present. All

because Father Beckingworth believed in him and wouldn't have wanted him to steal.

Bless Father Beckingworth.

Day Seven

Christmas is supposed to be a happy time at church. It's Christ's birthday, the beginning of all good things.

But it isn't a happy time. People get horribly depressed. Money is always tight for everyone in the parish and they get anxious. Husbands and wives fight with each other. Father Beckingworth has heard more confessions than he cares to remember this time of year about men yelling—or even swearing—at their wives in frustration. It must break Christ's heart that every year on his birthday men turn violent, women cower in fear, and adults all feel inadequate because they don't have enough money to buy their children everything they wanted. Sometimes they can't afford anything at all.

Children can't help but want gifts. That's all they see on television. One year Father Beckingworth thought it was a stroke of genius that he suggested that everyone in the parish shut off their televisions all during advent so they could do family things together instead of

being bombarded with ads on TV. Then the children wouldn't want so many things. Parents wouldn't feel so inadequate. His parishioners went for the idea. The first week everything went pretty well, and families came to church happy on Sunday.

But the next week things had started to fall apart. One family had decided to go out for walks in the evening and their baby girl had run off and slipped on the ice. She'd hit her head on the curb so hard she'd needed stitches. She'd had a bad concussion on top of that. Fortunately, she was all right after a stay in the hospital. The family didn't have insurance, though, so that had been a big problem.

The next week a house caught on fire when the family tried roasting chestnuts over a burner on their gas stove. One father decided it was a good time to teach his wife how to drive and she had almost immediately driven into a tow truck. Two brothers ran away from home when their mother made angel costumes for them and insisted they go up and down the street with her singing Christmas carols. An Amber alert had already been issued by the time they came home at midnight.

He'd called the whole no-watching-television idea off before the third week had gotten underway.

This year things are a little better. Mainly thanks to Sister Isabel and her brilliant way with children. She brings out the best in

them, can inspire them to do things they never dreamed of doing. This year, she's come up with a way to help parents afford gifts for their children. She asked her mother, a former dancer, to teach the children in the parish to dance.

"We will be so wonderful, hospitals and nightclubs all over the city will pay us $100 a night to perform. We'll use the money to start a Christmas store." Father Beckingworth hadn't thought it would work, but they've been booked solidly through the entire months of November and December. They've received rave reviews in the newspapers across the county.

Sister Isabel bought a room full of gifts with the money her dancers earned, and high school students struggling with math help run a store to sell the gifts to the parishioners. Everything costs less than a dollar, and each family is allowed to buy three things per family member.

Father Beckingworth can't imagine the math lessons Sister Isabel insists the store is providing will prove very valuable—the students will learn nothing more than a business will go broke selling things for less than it pays for them—but he likes the idea that they will learn "higher math"—the concept that happiness has no price.

He wants to do something for Sister Isabel, but what can he possibly do for a woman who has such heart and vision? He becomes obsessed with the thought that he must show his appreciation. He can't come up with any good ideas, and so he feels a failure.

Again, Christmas has brought him misery.

Even Gus, his most successful project to date, can't cheer him up, although he is almost moved to tears when the big man comes in all smiles and shyly gives him a fruitcake packed into a sweet, old-fashion tin. "The fruitcake is homemade, too. The real thing. Nothing but the best for you, Father Beckingworth."

And that's what he needs for Sister Isabel. The best.

Maybe eating a piece of the fruitcake will inspire him. At the very least, it'll take his mind off his inability to think of something nice to do for this angel of a nun.

He opens the tin, unwraps the cake, holds it to his nose, and inhales. He can't believe the aroma. It smells just like childhood. If only he could bottle such a sweet scent. That is what he would give Sister Isabel. He's never known anyone to love children as she does. To give her the scent of childhood would be the greatest gift in the world.

But again, he faces his limits. He is not a maker of perfume. He wouldn't even know how to scent one of the church's candles.

As he sets the fruitcake on a plate to slice it, he hears a knock on the rectory door. He leaves the cake on the table.

Sister Isabel steps in, holding out a package. "For you, Father."

He is devastated. Here is a saint giving him a present and he has nothing. He's worse than the drummer boy. He at least had a drum to beat.

"What is that lovely smell, Father?" Sister Isabel asks, heading toward his dining room. "It smells just like childhood."

He follows her, and as she leans over the fruitcake, his answer comes to him.

"Allow me to finish wrapping the fruitcake, Sister Isabel," he says. "The sweetness of childhood belongs to you."

It is the first time he has seen her cry.

Day Eight

Of all the children Sister Isabel has known, she has loved Melinda the best. Melinda is a fatherless child with a wheelchair-bound mother. They live in a one-room apartment that has two narrow beds, a table, and one chair. The bathroom is just big enough for the wheelchair. But Melinda never complains.

"We are so lucky," Melinda tells Sister Isabel as they leave the dance studio after a dress rehearsal. "We have a warm place to sleep. My mother's bed is low so I can easily help her get in it. She can get herself in and out of the bathroom by herself. Every night Wheels on Meals brings us food, so we have plenty to eat. I go to a wonderful school with wonderful people. I have you as my teacher, and I get to dance on a real stage!"

Melinda means every word she says. Sister Isabel has never encountered a spirit so pure and lovely. How she longs to give this angelic child something wonderful for Christmas, but Melinda's mother Betty is not nearly as sweet as Melinda.

In fact, she is a bitter lemon.

"She's my child," she hissed at Sister Isabel the first time they met and the nun praised Melinda. "Don't you dare try to tell me she's this or that or the other thing. You will never know her or love her like I do, so outside of your duties as a teacher and a nun, you stay away from her."

Sister Isabel knows Betty fears losing her daughter. Melinda is all she has. So she's careful never to give Betty a reason to worry.

Still, she would love to give Melinda a gift. She knows Betty will have nothing for her daughter and is too stubborn to take anything for the girl from anyone else. Melinda won't complain about a meager Christmas. She will find good in the holiday and has been making decorations for their apartment.

"Meals on Wheels will bring us a special dinner on Christmas," Melinda tells Sister Isabel. "Roast chicken and gravy. Stuffing, too. And not only pie, but also cake. And guess what? The Roberts heard our oven is broken. They live right next door and said we can use their oven to warm our dinner. It'll be piping hot! Isn't that great?"

Melinda is especially fond of St. Bernadette, who Melinda believes would cure her mother if only they had lived in the same day and age. Melinda prays to this saint daily. So when Sister Isabel finds a locket with St. Bernadette's image inside it, she uses some of the dance money to buy it for Melinda.

Up until now, she has not known how she would get it to her. The fruitcake is the answer.

Carefully, she cuts a small patch out of one side of the cake, slips the locket in, and replaces the patch.

"Melinda," she says on the last day of school, "I have a fruitcake for you and your mother. Someone gave it to me as a gift, and I am allergic to candied fruit, so I want you and your mother to enjoy it for me." She hopes God will forgive her for her small lie about the allergy.

"But —" Melinda begins.

"No buts," Sister Isabel insists. "Your mother will enjoy it. Think of that."

Melinda imagines it and smiles.

"Be careful when you bite into it," Sister Isabel says. "Sometimes bakers hide surprises in them."

Melinda laughs. "It's a surprise just to have it!" she says. "You are the nicest nun in the world. The nicest person, in fact."

Sister Isabel watches Melinda skip down the steps and across the school yard. It doesn't matter if it is Melinda or Betty who finds the necklace. Melinda will know that St. Bernadette has come to them and that everything is going to get better. It will give her more hope.

And hope is the one thing Melinda must always, always have.

Day Nine

Betty is angry. Melinda is late. There is always a reason to be angry with her daughter.

Melinda is too happy.

She tries too hard.

She's too cheerful.

She sleeps too soundly.

She's too helpful.

She's too perfect.

But mostly, she exists.

And Betty can't give her what she deserves.

Melinda is a constant reminder of Betty's failures. She couldn't even stay healthy. She hadn't been smart enough or deserving enough to marry a man who believed in for better or for worse.

While Betty seethes with anger, Melinda oozes excitement. She actually has a gift for her mother. One she'll love. She won't be mad at her this time. Her mother loves British mysteries. Melinda reads

them to her at night, and her mother especially likes the part about the teas. Everyone in British mysteries drinks lots of tea.

On the way home, Melinda stops at the corner store. She's been saving her milk money for something special for her mother, and she has just enough to buy a colorful box full of tea bags. She tucks the tea bags safely into her backpack, just beside her fruitcake.

Before she goes into her apartment, she stops at the apartment across the stairwell from hers. Lisa lives there. She always helps when Melinda or her mother needs something and comes to the rescue without being asked. Melinda isn't sure she should interrupt whatever Lisa is doing to ask a favor. She could be busy studying.

But Lisa doesn't mind the interruption. She puts water on to boil and rummages through a cupboard for a teapot she's tucked away. Its pattern has faded into cracks and its spout is chipped. Lisa is disappointed by the state of the teapot, but Melinda thinks it's perfect.

"I never dreamed I might be able to serve my mother tea in a genuine teapot," she says, her cheeks rosy with pleasure. "Tomorrow I'll bring you a piece of fruitcake."

Lisa insists on pouring the boiling water into the teapot so Melinda doesn't scald herself. Then with her backpack tucked under her arm, Melinda carries the teapot in both hands to her apartment. She will make her mother tea. She and her mother will eat fruitcake. An English tea.

It will be a special evening, a Holy Week night to remember. She unlocks the door and lets herself in, leaving the teapot and backpack holding the tea bags and fruitcake in the hallway.

"Melinda! You're late! I've been worried sick!"

"I have a surprise for us, Mommy."

"I don't want a surprise. I want to be able to count on you."

Melinda sets two mismatched mugs and two chipped plates on the table. She's careful to keep her back turned to her mother so her mother won't worry that she's made her cry.

Her mother loves her, but she can't help getting angry with her sometimes. Then her mother gets angry with herself for getting angry and it's all a big mess. But Melinda won't let that happen tonight. They love each other, and they will have a fine English tea together.

Betty watches her slight, beautiful daughter set the table. Her heart swells with love. She is so lucky to have a daughter. Without her, she would be all alone. How she wishes she wouldn't yell at her. How she wishes she could show her love instead of needing her care. A mother should be able to care for her child. It shouldn't be the other way around. She wants to give her a gift, but how? She has no money.

"Close your eyes, Mommy," Melinda says.

Betty listens to her daughter open the door. She wonders what she is bringing in. A kitten? Oh please, not a kitten. She knows her daughter wants one more than anything, but how will they feed it?

She feels her daughter's touch on her shoulders for a brief moment before she slides her hands to the handles on the back of the wheelchair. She keeps her eyes closed as Melinda wheels her to the table.

"Open your eyes now," Melinda says.

Betty can't figure out at first what Melinda has done.

"Tea, Mommy. Just like in your books."

Melinda pours the hot water into the cups and lets the tea bags turn the water into tea. She lifts the lid off the fruitcake. "And cake to go with it."

"You are the sweetest child in the world," Betty tells her. Overwhelmed with emotion, she pushes her chair back and pulls her daughter into a hug. Melinda loses her balance and falls into her mother's lap. They sit that way until the tea turns lukewarm, the perfect picture of a mother holding her child.

When Betty finally releases her, Melinda says, "Would you like your cake now?"

Betty shakes her head. "Not just yet," she says. "Let's keep it and think about it a bit longer, shall we?"

"Sure," Melinda says. She is still warm from her mother's embrace. They can wait for days as far as she's concerned. Her mother is smiling. She can always reheat the tea. Inside, a fire lights them both.

Day Ten

Betty sends Melinda out for bread. "Make sure it's fresh," she reminds her.

She watches out the window until Melinda turns the corner. She takes a deep breath and opens the door. The dark hallway terrifies her. What if her wheelchair catches on something, throwing her out of it? She couldn't get up on her own. She could be in pain for hours.

But she can do this. She must do this.

The ominous staircase looms there, just ahead, running down the middle of the hallway. She has to pass it to get to Lisa's apartment. The old wheelchair doesn't maneuver well at all. One slip and she'll tumble down, down, down those hard, pitted steps. She wishes she lived on the ground floor, but she's been on the waiting list for almost three years now. Her heart pounds as she inches down the hallway, the threadbare carpet bunching under her wheels, making progress difficult. She should turn back. Stay in the apartment where it's safe.

How will she feed a kitten, anyway? Where will the money come from? They hardly have enough as it is.

She can still smell her daughter's strawberry shampoo. She can picture her smiling blue eyes. She thinks of how Melinda giggles in her sleep. Of how she felt cuddled up on her lap the night before.

Slowly, slowly, she edges out into the hall. She can do this. For Melinda.

She hates asking favors of anyone, but she will overcome that for her daughter. Besides, Lisa seems nice. She's come over a couple of times with candles when the electricity went out. Once they were snowed in for three days, and Lisa made sure Betty and Melinda were all right, giving them tips on staying warm and sharing her canned tuna with them.

Once Melinda asked Lisa how she knew how to do so many things without electricity. Lisa had replied, "Oh, I've been taking care of things on my own since I was littler than you. Guess I just picked things up along the way."

Lisa keeps to herself for the most part. She doesn't seem to have any family, and as far as Betty knows, Lisa doesn't have any visitors. But if she can put herself through college, she'll know how to take care of things. If anyone can help her, Betty reasons, Lisa can.

"Be home, Lisa," she pleads aloud. "Please, please. Be home."

Lisa opens the door moments after Betty knocks.

"I'm wondering if you could do something for me," Betty says, swallowing the tiny bit of pride she has left. "It would be a big favor. I'd like to get my daughter a kitten, but I can't get out to find her one. I'm wondering if you can help. I want to give it to her for Christmas."

Lisa thinks for a minute. It's not good to get too involved with people. Keep your distance and you're safe enough. Get close, and they'll find out you're nothing but a selfish sow. Her mother pointed out Lisa's selfishness from the time she was a little girl, and she can't bear having anyone else know this horrible truth about her.

"My daughter is such a good child and she's wanted a kitten since, well, since forever, I think. We can manage one somehow, I believe."

Lisa might not know what it's like to be a good child, but she knows what it's like to be a child who wants something. She can still hear her mother's accusations that if Lisa's didn't need so many things, she might be able to afford something nice for herself. Her mother would work herself up until she decided Lisa was an ungrateful child who didn't deserve anything at all, and then her mother would treat herself to something special for herself. Why shouldn't she? She was the one who worked her fingers to a bone putting food on the table.

Pausing to assess the situation, Lisa marvels that this mother wants her daughter to be happy. That must mean Melinda deserves things. She wants to help, but it's risky letting someone into your life. But Melinda is thoughtful. Just the night before she had planned that

English tea for her mother. How can she say no to helping Betty find a kitten for her?

Lisa thinks quickly. She can always just get the kitten and go back about her business. It's not kitten season, but still, she can probably find one. In fact, she even has a cat dish and a litter box they could have. Her mother had thrown it out the window at her when Lisa had finally found out where her mother was living and had gone to visit her.

"Any particular color kitten?" Lisa asks.

They talk very briefly—Betty is afraid Melinda will come home.

Betty holds out the fruitcake. "I'm afraid I can't pay you, but I'd like you to take this for your trouble."

"Oh, there's no need for that," Lisa says, shaking her head. She doesn't deserve any payment. Not a selfish person like her. "It's okay."

"You don't understand," Betty tells her. "If you don't take something for doing this for me, then the kitten is your present and not mine. Please. It is all I have to give."

Lisa considers the situation. She doesn't like to take anything from anyone. It is a selfish thing to do. But Betty's eyes are so pleading that she reaches out for the tin. "Thank you," Lisa says. "I love fruitcake. But I don't deserve such kindness."

Quickly, before Melinda comes back to the apartment, Betty returns to their room. She flashes a triumphant look at the formidable

staircase. She's faced it, and in that knowledge a seed is planted. Maybe it's safe to leave the apartment after all. She doesn't have to go far. Just a little further every day. There's an elevator at the far end of the hallway. It hasn't ever been stuck between floors when other tenants have used it. If she keeps track of the elevator to make sure it continues to be safe, maybe by summer she will be brave enough to use it, too. If she can do that, the next step will be to go outside. Maybe she can even make it as far as the training center the social worker keeps bringing up during her visits. That could lead to a job. To a real income. To a better life for her and Melinda.

It's a small seed, but it's been planted. Strength nearly bursts out of Betty's limbs.

Day Eleven

Lisa hides the kitten in her locker at the coffee shop. She puts a chair against it so the kitten won't be able to slip out, leaving just a tiny crack open so the kitty will have fresh air. The kitten is a perfect little ball of calico fluff.

She hopes Betty will let her watch Melinda's excitement when she first meets the kitten. She wouldn't mind getting to know them a little. She'll be careful not to intrude. She won't monopolize their time. Maybe she'll just invite them over now and then to play cards. She'll let them win. She'll serve sandwiches and tangerines. Sometimes it's good to do something nice for someone. Even somebody as horrid and selfish as she is knows that.

She is going to give that fruitcake to Arella, the old woman who comes in once a week for coffee. Arella seems to be all alone in the world, the kind of woman who might appreciate an unexpected gift. Lisa can tell by Arella's baggy faded red coat that she doesn't have

much money, but yet she always leaves her a dollar tip, which is more than the cup of coffee she orders.

"College is expensive," Arella always tells her. "And you're an industrious girl to work your way through school all on your own. I admire you for that. And I just know your hard work is going to pay off."

Lisa knows Arella won't accept a free cup of coffee for fear it would get Lisa in trouble, but how can she say no to a fruitcake? Especially one in such a lovely old tin. It looks to be an antique.

The old woman shows up at 9:35 on the dot. Just like always.

They chat for a bit as Arella settles in and orders her coffee. The woman is full of questions. She asks Lisa about school, what she'll do during Christmas break, what classes she'll take next semester. Lisa imagines her own grandmother would have asked her the same questions. But she's never had a grandmother as far as she knows. It's nice to have a sort-of-grandmother now. Kind of a fairy grandmother, really.

When Arella finishes her coffee and slips Lisa a dollar—which is actually a twenty dollar bill Lisa will find out later—under her cup, Lisa helps her into her coat.

"Oh!" says Lisa. "Wait! I have something for you." If she acts like it's a big deal, Arella might turn her down. Then they'd both be embarrassed and it would ruin everything. What if she didn't come

by anymore? Not having a grandmother is bad enough, losing your fairy grandmother would be unthinkable. She hesitates a moment as she wonders if this is selfish thinking.

But no, Lisa will not let the echoes of her mother's taunts ruin this. She hurriedly hands Arella the fruitcake. "Just a little something to go with your coffee on the days you have your coffee at home." The words tumble out of her mouth so quickly they all run together, but Arella understands.

And then Arella does the most amazing thing—she wraps her arms around Lisa and hugs her close. "What a thoughtful, generous young woman you are," she says. "If I had a granddaughter, I'd want her to be just like you."

By spring Lisa will find out that Arella has an uncanny ability to find scholarships and grants that seem custom made for her. She finds so many, in fact, that when Lisa begins a career at a homeless shelter for teenagers in two years, she will not owe so much as a dime in student loans.

Day Twelve

Arella opens her tin and inhales the aroma, made sweeter by the passage of both time and hands. She lifts the fruitcake from the tin, puts it on a silver plate, and holds her fingers over it to feel its moistness rise like a cloud.

"Tell me," she whispers to her fruitcake, "Where have you gone? What have you seen?" She closes her eyes and listens.

Later she will cut two thick slices from the cake and take them to Bea's apartment for a Christmas Eve snack. Bea will find the St. Bernadette locket in her slice, and almost immediately, she will feel remarkably better.

The End

Acknowledgements

Thank you to my parents who always made Christmas magical, to my children who continue that tradition, and to Anne Lawrence, Gay Lynn Bath, and Christie Holmgren for their support as I shaped this tale.

Made in the USA
Columbia, SC
18 December 2021

52088583R00039